This book belongs to:

....

(You!)

Twirlywoos and all related titles, logos and characters are trademarks of DHX Worldwide Ltd
© 2017 Ragdoll Productions Ltd/DHX Worldwide Ltd
Some images © Shutterstock

Written by Stella Gurney
Designed by Anna Lubecka

First published in the UK in 2017 by HarperCollins Children's Books.
HarperCollins Children's Books is a division of HarperCollins Publishers Ltd,
1 London Bridge Street, London, SE1 9GF
1 3 5 7 9 10 8 6 4 2
ISBN: 978-0-00-821973-4

MIX
Paper from
responsible sources
FSC **FSC™ C007454**
www.fsc.org

FSC ™ is a non-profit international organisation established to promo
the responsible management of the world's forests. Products carrying
FSC label are independently certified to assure consumers that they cc
from forests that are managed to meet the social, economic and
ecological needs of present and future generations,
and other controlled sources.

Find out more about HarperCollins and the environment at
www.harpercollins.co.uk/green

It's the Twirlywoos!

Great BigHoo!

Toodloo!

Chickedy!

Chick!

Today they're learning something new.
All about... **noisy!**

Toot!
Toot!

Off they go,
into the clouds.

What's
this?

It's a **radio**.

Great BigHoo
tries to turn it off.
He presses
a button.

It makes the radio even NOISIER!

Hoo!

And now
somebody's
coming!

The lady
presses
a button and
the music stops.

Ahhh...
that's
better.

ZzzZzzZzzz

The lady settles in her chair for a nap.

What are Chickedy and Chick doing?

Noisy!

Time to go, Twirlywoos. Let's see what else you can find that's noisy.

A drill - **noisy!**

A barking dog - **noisy!**

An aeroplane - **noisy!**

A megaphone - **noisy!**

Fireworks - **noisy!**

Can **you** make any of these noises, too?

What else is **noisy?**

A cockerel –
noisy!

Drums – **noisy!**

A big lorry - **noisy!**

A trumpet - **noisy!**

Popping popcorn - **noisy!**

Knock!

Knock!

Knock!

And what's *that* noise?

There's somebody at the door.

It's **The Stop-Go Car.**

Beep!

Beep!

Beep! Beep!

Too noisy!

Beep! Beep! Beep!

Bye-bye,
Stop-Go
Car!

Time for some Fruit Tea. There's
The Fruit Tea Machine.

What flavour
is the Fruit
Tea today?

The Twirlywoos are drinking their Fruit Tea.

SLurp! SLurp! SLurp! SLurp! SLurp!

Very noisy!

Here come the **Twirly Rings.**

Jump in,
Twirlywoos.

Time to go.

Bye-bye,
Twirlywoos!

Discover more amazing TWIRLYWOOS books!

 Meet the Twirlywoos!

 Hello, Chickedy! Hello, Chick!

 Upside Down

 Gone!

 Wrapping!

 In and Out

 It's the Twirlywoos! Sticker Activity Book
Packed with Twirlywoos stickers!

 Wipe Clean Activity Book
With a special Twirlywoos pen!

 Colouring Book
Colour in the Twirlywoos!

 Happy Easter Twirlywoos Sticker Activity Book
With over 150 stickers!

 Collecting

 The Big Red Boat

 Meet the Twirlywoos!

 Little Library

 I can do that too, Twirlywoos!